WINGS OF FIRE

THE DRAGONET PROPHECY
THE GRAPHIC NOVEL

For Jonah, my little bigwings.
—T.T.S.

This book is dedicated, as always and forever,
to Meredith, and to our pets, Heidi the dog and
Ella the cat, whose personalities and poses can
be found all throughout this book.
—M.H.

Story and text copyright © 2018 by Tui T. Sutherland
Adaptation by Barry Deutsch
Map and border design © 2012 by Mike Schley
Art by Mike Holmes © 2018 by Scholastic Inc.

Library of Congress Control Number Available

ISBN 978-0-545-94216-4 (hardcover)
ISBN 978-0-545-94215-7 (paperback)

32 31 30 29 28 27 26 25   22 23 24 25 26

Printed in Mexico   189
First edition, January 2018
Edited by Amanda Maciel
Lettering by John Green
Book design by Phil Falco
Creative Director: David Saylor

TUI T. SUTHERLAND

ART BY MIKE HOLMES

WINGS OF FIRE

THE GRAPHIC NOVEL

BOOK ONE
THE DRAGONET PROPHECY

SCHOLASTIC

WINGS OF FIRE

THE DRAGONET PROPHECY
THE GRAPHIC NOVEL

BY TUI T. SUTHERLAND

ADAPTED BY BARRY DEUTSCH
ART BY MIKE HOLMES
COLOR BY MAARTA LAIHO

AN IMPRINT OF
SCHOLASTIC

Queen Glacier's Palace

Ice Kingdom

Sky Kingdom

Burn's Stronghold

Under the Mountain

Kingdom of Sand

Scorpion Den

Jade Mountain

Queen Scarlet's
Palace

Diamond Spray River

Kingdom of
the Sea

Diamond Spray
Delta

Mud Kingdom

Scavenger
Den

Scavenger Den

Rainforest Kingdom

THE DRAGONET
PROPHECY

WHEN THE WAR HAS LASTED TWENTY YEARS...
THE DRAGONETS WILL COME.
   WHEN THE LAND IS SOAKED IN BLOOD AND TEARS...
    THE DRAGONETS WILL COME.

 FIND THE SEAWING EGG OF DEEPEST BLUE,
  WINGS OF NIGHT SHALL COME TO YOU.

      THE LARGEST EGG IN MOUNTAIN HIGH
        WILL GIVE TO YOU THE WINGS OF SKY.

     FOR WINGS OF EARTH, SEARCH THROUGH THE MUD
      FOR AN EGG THE COLOR OF DRAGON BLOOD.
        AND HIDDEN ALONE FROM THE RIVAL QUEENS,
         THE SANDWING EGG AWAITS UNSEEN.

Of three queens who blister and blaze and burn
Two shall die and one shall learn
If she bows to a fate that is stronger and higher,
She'll have the power of wings of fire.

Five eggs to hatch on brightest night,
Five dragons born to end the fight.
Darkness will rise to bring the light.
The dragonets are coming...

ARE ALL MUDWINGS THIS USELESS, OR JUST *YOU?*

FIND THE MONSTER INSIDE YOU! LET IT OUT!

AAAAAH!

STOP PICKING ON CLAY!

TSUNAMI. AREN'T YOU SWEET? PROTECTING A DRAGON WHO TRIED TO *KILL* YOU IN YOUR EGG.

BUT LUCKILY YOU BIG DRAGONS WERE THERE TO *SAVE* OUR *LIVES.*

AND NOW WE GET TO HEAR ABOUT IT ALL *THE TIME.*

WE'RE FINISHED ANYWAY. ANOTHER UNIMPRESSIVE SESSION, MUDWING.

SHE'S GOING TO BE SO MEAN TO YOU DURING TRAINING TOMORROW.

OH NO! HOW UNEXPECTED! I'VE *NEVER* SEEN KESTREL BE MEAN BEFORE!

HA HA! OWWWW.

KESTREL WILL BE SORRY ONE DAY, WHEN I'M QUEEN OF THE SEAWINGS.

I THOUGHT ONLY A QUEEN'S DAUGHTERS OR SISTERS COULD CHALLENGE HER FOR THE THRONE.

WELL, MAYBE THE SEAWING QUEEN *IS* MY MOTHER AND I'M A LOST PRINCESS.

I WONDER WHAT MY PARENTS ARE LIKE.

I WONDER IF ANY OF OUR PARENTS ARE STILL ALIVE.

YOU THINK THEY EVER MISS US?

DEFINITELY. I BET THEY TORE UP THE WORLD LOOKING FOR US.

THE TALONS OF PEACE HID US WELL. BUT...

BUT WHAT?

BUT WHAT IF WE ESCAPE?

I'M READY TO SAVE THE WORLD NOW. AREN'T YOU?

UM, NO. WE CAN'T STOP THE WAR BY OURSELVES.

YES, WE CAN! THAT'S THE WHOLE *POINT* OF THE PROPHECY.

JUST THINK ABOUT IT, OK?

ALL RIGHT. I'LL THINK ABOUT IT.

MOOOO.

MOOOOO!

MOOOOO.

DINNER!

RACE YOU!

DINNER! COWS! *HOORAY!*

OBVIOUSLY, I'D BE THE BEST QUEEN, BUT SUNNY CAN PLAY QUEEN OASIS SINCE SHE'S A REAL SANDWING.

CLAY, YOU'RE THE SCAVENGER. THIS CAN BE YOUR CLAW.

AND THE REST OF US WILL BE PRINCESSES. I'LL BE *BURN*, THE STRONG ONE, OBVIOUSLY.

GLORY, YOU'RE *BLISTER*, THE SMART ONE.

AND STARFLIGHT, YOU CAN BE *BLAZE*, THE ONE THE SANDWINGS LIKE.

THE PRETTY ONE.

I HAD TO BE BLAZE LAST TIME, TOO.

STOP COMPLAINING.

HOW THE GREAT WAR BEGAN

THEN THEY PICK THEIR ALLIANCES AND ALL THAT BORING STUFF.

BORING? SURELY YOU MEAN *ESSENTIAL TO FULFILLING THE PROPHECY.*

OH, GO AHEAD. IT'S NOT LIKE WE CAN STOP YOU!

WE KNOW THIS IS YOUR FAVORITE PART.

FINE.

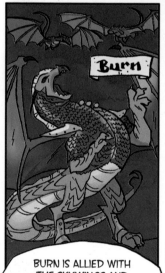

Burn

BURN IS ALLIED WITH THE SKYWINGS AND MUDWINGS. SHE COULD CRUSH THE OTHERS LIKE BUGS IN CLAW-TO-CLAW COMBAT. IF SHE WINS, SHE'LL PROBABLY KEEP THE WAR GOING JUST FOR FUN.

Blister

BLISTER'S ALLIED WITH THE SEAWINGS. SHE'S SMARTER THAN THE OTHER TWO PUT TOGETHER.

SMART SOUNDS GOOD.

SHE'S ALSO CONNIVING. IF SHE WINS, SHE'LL PROBABLY TRY TO TAKE OVER THE OTHER TRIBES. IT WAS HER IDEA TO START THE WAR, SINCE SHE KNEW SHE COULDN'T KILL BURN IN A REGULAR DUEL FOR THE THRONE.

Blaze

BLAZE IS THE SANDWING FAVORITE.

SO WHY CAN'T SHE BE QUEEN?

BURN WOULD DESTROY HER.

ALSO, BLAZE IS ABOUT AS SMART AS A CONCUSSED SHEEP.

THANK YOU SO MUCH, TSUNAMI, FOR ALWAYS MAKING ME PLAY HER.

YOU'RE WELCOME.

WE HAVE TO PICK ONE, RIGHT? WHEN WE FULFILL THE PROPHECY? WHO DO WE CHOOSE WHEN THEY'RE ALL SO TERRIBLE?

I DON'T KNOW.

WHOSE SIDE ARE THE NIGHTWINGS ON?

A NIGHTWING CALLED MORROWSEER WROTE OUR PROPHECY, BUT THEY'RE NOT INVOLVED IN THE WAR.

BECAUSE THEY'RE *SOOOO* POWERFUL. AND *SOOOOO* MYSTERIOUS.

IF THEY CAN SEE THE FUTURE, THEY MUST KNOW WHO WINS.

I'M NOT SURE IT WORKS LIKE THAT—

THEY COULD JUST *TELL* EVERYONE ALREADY SO WE CAN GO HOME.

WHAT ABOUT THE RAINWINGS?

THEY'RE NOT INVOLVED EITHER.

WHO WOULD WANT THE RAINWINGS AS ALLIES?

LISTEN TO KESTREL SOMETIME.

WE'RE ALL TOO LAZY AND TOO STUPID.

YOU'RE NOT STUPID OR LAZY.

THE GUARDIANS DON'T REALLY MEAN IT. YOU'RE A DRAGONET OF DESTINY! I'M SURE THEY BELIEVE IN YOU!

ER... SUNNY, YOU KNOW THAT WEIRD BUG YOU CAUGHT AT DINNER? CAN YOU BRING IT HERE TO SHOW STARFLIGHT?

HE SAW IT AT DINNER—

NO, HE WAS READING. RIGHT, STARFLIGHT?

YEAH, I DIDN'T SEE IT.

YOU *GOTTA* SEE IT! IT'S *SO* WEIRD!

I CAN'T STAND THIS MUCH LONGER. WE HAVE TO GET OUT OF HERE. SOON.

YOU TALKED TO THEM ABOUT IT?

OF COURSE. I NEEDED THEIR HELP FIGURING OUT AN ESCAPE PLAN.

I'M NOT SURE WE'RE READY. THERE'S SO MUCH WE HAVEN'T LEARNED YET...

WE NEVER WILL UNTIL WE SEE THE WORLD FOR OURSELVES!

WHAT ABOUT THE PROPHECY? SHOULDN'T WE WAIT UNTIL OUR GUARDIANS SAY IT'S TIME?

I DON'T SEE WHY. I'M WITH TSUNAMI.

DESTINY IS DESTINY, SO WHATEVER WE DO MUST BE RIGHT. WE DON'T NEED A BUNCH OF ANCIENT DRAGONS TELLING US HOW TO SAVE THE WORLD. *THEY'RE* NOT IN THE PROPHECY.

WHEN DO WE TELL SUNNY?

NOT UNTIL THE LAST MINUTE. YOU KNOW SHE CAN'T KEEP A SECRET.

THAT'S THE ENTRANCE BOULDER!

THIS LATE AT NIGHT? SOMETHING'S HAPPENING.

CRASH!

I'M SURE THEY'LL TELL US WHAT'S GOING ON TOMORROW.

DON'T BE A SMOKE-BREATHER. LET'S GO!

CLAY, COME ON —WE CAN SPY ON THEM FROM THE RIVER.

COMING *HERE*? WITH NO WARNING? AFTER SIX YEARS, HE'S SUDDENLY INTERESTED?

WELL, IT IS HIS PROPHECY. I GUESS HE WANTS TO MAKE SURE THEY CAN ACTUALLY STOP THE WAR.

HIS PROPHECY?

THEY'RE TALKING ABOUT MORROWSEER!

THESE DRAGONETS? THEN HE'S GOING TO BE VERY DISAPPOINTED.

WE'VE DONE OUR BEST. THE PROPHECY CHOSE THEM, NOT US.

DO YOU THINK MORROWSEER'S COMING TO TAKE US OUT OF HERE?

MAYBE?

DOES HE EVEN KNOW WHAT HAPPENED? DOES HE KNOW ABOUT THE DEFECTIVE SANDWING, OR THAT *YOU* BROUGHT US A *RAINWING*?

HE CAN'T COMPLAIN ABOUT SUNNY. WE FOLLOWED THE PROPHECY. AND GLORY'S NOT THAT BAD. SHE'S SMARTER THAN SHE WANTS US TO KNOW.

SHE'S AS LAZY AND WORTHLESS AS ANY OTHER RAINWING.

AND SHE'S NOT A SKYWING. WE'RE *SUPPOSED* TO HAVE A SKYWING.

HE'S HERE. HE'S HERE!

ARE YOU MORROWSEER? CAN YOU GET US OUT OF HERE?

HUSH, YOU UNGRATEFUL LIZARD!

WHAT.

IS.

THAT?

THERE WAS AN ACCIDENT. WE LOST THE SKYWING EGG, SO WE HAD TO GET ANOTHER SOMEWHERE AND —

FROM THE RAINWINGS?

HE BROUGHT HER HERE.

WE HAVE FIVE DRAGONETS. THAT'S WHAT MATTERS.

MORE LIKE FOUR AND A HALF. ARE YOU SUPPOSED TO BE THE SANDWING? DON'T YOU EAT? WHAT'S WRONG WITH YOU?

SHE EATS! AND SHE'S A GOOD FIGHTER.

IT'S NOT HER FAULT SHE'S SMALL.

GLORY'S A GOOD FIGHTER, TOO.

WE NEED A PLAN.

BUT NIGHTWINGS CAN READ MINDS!

THINK ABOUT COWS.

HE'LL KNOW ANY PLAN I MAKE.

UNLESS I DON'T THINK ABOUT IT...

COWS! COWS!

OUCH!

HA! THAT'S A SURPRISE.

SEE? SUNNY IS A GOOD FIGHTER. FIERCE AND BRAVE.

WHY DIDN'T THE GUARDIANS TRY TO HELP US?

HMM.

THIS ONE... WE'LL HAVE TO SEE.

THESE TWO WILL DO.

I ASSUME *YOU* USED YOUR NIGHTWING POWERS TO SEE I WASN'T GOING TO HARM THE SEAWING. NO DOUBT YOU ALSO ALREADY KNOW I'M GOING TO TAKE YOU INTO THE NEXT CAVERN FOR A PRIVATE CONVERSATION.

AS FOR THE RAINWING...

WE'LL TALK ABOUT *HER* LATER.

HOW DARE YOU COMPLAIN ABOUT US?

IF IT WASN'T MY JOB TO KEEP YOU ALIVE, I'D HAVE STRANGLED YOU *MYSELF* A LONG TIME AGO.

I ONLY TOLD HIM THE TRUTH.

YUP. AND I FAILED IT THE DAY I HATCHED AS A RAINWING.

WELL, WE DON'T CARE WHAT THE PROPHECY SAYS OR WHAT MORROWSEER THINKS. YOU'RE OUR FIFTH DRAGONET.

YOU'RE SWEET. I'M GOING TO TAKE A NAP.

A NAP? IS THAT A GOOD IDEA RIGHT NOW?

THEY ALL THINK I'M LAZY ANYWAY.

NOTHING I DO CAN CHANGE THAT.

WAKE ME IF ANYTHING EXCITING HAPPENS.

BUT MAKE SURE IT'S ACTUALLY EXCITING, NOT SUNNY-EXCITING.

HOW COULD THE PROPHECY NOT INCLUDE GLORY?

HMPH!

I DON'T THINK *EVERYTHING* IS EXCITING! BUT YOU GUYS DON'T THINK *ENOUGH* THINGS ARE EXCITING.

SUNNY. WHAT WOULD YOU THINK ABOUT RUNNING AWAY?

YOU MEAN LEAVING THE CAVES? WITHOUT OUR GUARDIANS? OH, NO, WE COULDN'T.

WE HAVE TO DO WHAT THE PROPHECY SAYS. THE TALONS UNDERSTAND IT. AS LONG AS WE FOLLOW IT, EVERYTHING WILL BE OKAY.

YEAH.

YOU'RE PROBABLY RIGHT.

BUT WHAT IF THE PROPHECY IS WRONG?

STARFLIGHT!

WHAT DID HE SAY TO YOU? ARE YOU ALL RIGHT?

I'M NOT SUPPOSED TO TALK ABOUT IT.

I... HAVE A LOT TO LEARN.

BUT YOU ALREADY KNOW EVERYTHING! YOU'RE THE SMARTEST DRAGONET IN PYRRHIA!

IT'S OVER HERE.

HIS FAVORITE SCROLL. HE REALLY *IS* UPSET.

I THOUGHT HE LIKED YOU. MORE THAN THE REST OF US ANYWAY. DIDN'T HE SAY WHAT A GREAT AND NOBLE DRAGON YOU MUST BE BECAUSE YOU'RE A NIGHTWING?

THAT'S EXACTLY WHAT HE TOLD ME, ACTUALLY.

WHAT ARE YOU DOING? LET HER GO!

THERE HAVE TO BE FIVE OF THEM. WHAT'S HE PLANNING TO DO ABOUT THAT?

HE'LL FIND US A SKYWING. LIKE WE **SHOULD** HAVE HAD IN THE FIRST PLACE.

DROWNING WOULD BE SIMPLEST.

I JOINED THE TALONS OF PEACE TO **STOP** KILLING DRAGONS. I WON'T ARGUE WITH MORROWSEER. BUT I'M NOT DOING IT.

HA. NO ONE EXPECTED **YOU** TO BE ANY USE.

IT HAS TO BE ME. I'M THE STRONGEST.

CAN YOU GO THROUGH WITH IT? AFTER WHAT HAPPENED TO —

GLORY'S JUST A RAINWING. I'LL DO IT TONIGHT WHILE SHE'S SLEEPING. TSUNAMI'S THE ONLY ONE WHO COULD HAVE STOPPED ME.

CLAY WILL TRY. HE'S DUMB AS A ROCK, BUT HE'LL DO ANYTHING FOR THOSE FOUR.

IT'S NOT NATURAL. DRAGONS SHOULDN'T BE THAT LOYAL OUTSIDE THEIR TRIBE.

I CAN HANDLE CLAY.

EVEN IF HE FINALLY LETS OUT THE MONSTER INSIDE, THERE'S NOTHING HE CAN DO.

GLORY WILL BE DEAD BY MORNING.

THIS IS ALL REALLY SWEET, GUYS, BUT DON'T GET IN TROUBLE FOR ME.

ACTING LIKE A MARTYR ISN'T HELPING THINGS.

I'M NOT *ACTING LIKE A MARTYR.* I'M TRYING TO MAKE SURE NOBODY GETS *KILLED.*

OH, BUT IT'S FINE IF *YOU* DO?

WHO *CARES?* I'M NOT IN THE PROPHECY!

I SWEAR I'LL KILL YOU MYSELF.

GLORY, SHE'S SAYING *WE* CARE!

GUYS! *LISTEN!* WHAT ABOUT THE SKY HOLE? IN THE STUDY ROOM? WE COULD FLY UP AND SQUEEZE OUT!

IT'S TOO SMALL, EVEN FOR YOU. I'VE FLOWN UP TO THE HOLE WHEN NO ONE WAS AROUND.

ME TOO.

ME TOO.

WHY DIDN'T *I* EVER TRY THAT?

YOU HAVE AN IDEA. I CAN TELL. YOU'VE BEEN WORKING ON AN ESCAPE PLAN FOREVER.

FOREVER? WHY DIDN'T ANYONE TELL ME?

IT'S TOO DANGEROUS. IT WAS SUPPOSED TO BE ME.

THE RIVER?

DO YOU KNOW WHERE IT GOES?

I FOUND A GAP UNDER THE WALL IN THE TRAINING CAVE. IT'S VERY TIGHT. I'VE NEVER GONE THROUGH IN CASE I COULDN'T GET BACK.

I'LL GO. WITH YOU TIED UP, I'M THE BEST SWIMMER.

CLAY, YOU CAN'T!

MUDWINGS CAN ONLY HOLD THEIR BREATH FOR AN HOUR—YOU COULD GET TRAPPED WITH NO AIR AND DROWN. AND YOU CAN'T SEE IN THE DARK LIKE I CAN. YOU COULD DIE!

GLORY **WILL** DIE IF I DON'T. RIGHT? THERE'S NO OTHER WAY.

YOU DON'T EVEN HAVE TO RISK THE RIVER, CLAY. I COULD JUST STAY LIKE THIS.

FOR HOW LONG? UNTIL YOU STARVE?

THEY'RE TRYING TO *KILL* YOU. WE HAVE TO GET OUT.

ALL RIGHT. DO WHAT YOU WANT.

AS LONG AS YOU'RE NOT JUST DOING IT FOR ME.

BE REALLY, REALLY CAREFUL, CLAY.

FOLLOW THE CURRENT. IF THE RIVER GOES OUT INTO THE WORLD ANYWHERE, THE CURRENT WILL TAKE YOU THERE.

IF?

DON'T PANIC. DON'T PANIC. DON'T—

I'LL HAVE TO APPROACH THE WATERFALL SLOWLY AND CARE—

AAAAAAAH!

DON'T PANIC DON'T PANIC DON'T—

WATCH OUT, CLAY! IT'S REALLY DANGEROUS! YOU MIGHT STUB A CLAW!

WHATEVER YOU DO, DON'T LET GO!

HA. HA.

C'MON. THE EXIT'S THIS WAY.

HOW DID YOU GET HERE?

WHO ARE YOU?

HOW CAN YOU NOT KNOW THAT?

YOU'RE NOT A VERY GOOD SPY, ARE YOU, SEAWING?

I'M *NOT* A SPY! WE'VE BEEN — HELD PRISONER, KIND OF. WE JUST ESCAPED!

A SEAWING AND A MUDWING HELD PRISONER? BUT YOU'RE NOT FROM MY DUNGEONS, UNLESS I'M GETTING HORRIBLY FORGETFUL. SO WHO *COULD* YOU BE?

TSUNAMI, COME ON. JUST GIVE BACK HER TREASURE AND LET'S GO.

THE QUEEN OF THE SKYWINGS!

NOW *YOU*, MUDWING, MAKE ME CURIOUS. WE'RE ON THE SAME SIDE. SO *WHY* DIDN'T YOU RECOGNIZE ME?

I DON'T—WE'RE JUST PASSING THROUGH—I MEAN—IT WAS AN HONOR TO MEET— *WE HAVE TO GO!*

BUT YOU *CAN'T* ABANDON ME MIDCONVERSATION. I KNOW—I'LL BRING YOU BACK TO MY SKY PALACE WITH ME. WON'T THAT BE THRILLING?

AAAAAH!

HOW *DARE* YOU?

NOW, REALLY, THIS IS GETTING INSULTING. YOU'RE IN *MY* TERRITORY. HOW *DARE* YOU NOT RECOGNIZE ME?

QUEEN SCARLET OF THE SKYWINGS.

YOU'RE A NIGHTWING! HOW *THRILLING!* I'VE NEVER HAD A NIGHTWING IN MY ARENA BEFORE.

TELL ME, WHAT AM I THINKING RIGHT NOW?

TOO HARD?

I'LL GIVE YOU A HINT.

WHY WOULD A NIGHTWING, A SEAWING, A MUDWING, AND... *WHATEVER* THOSE TWO ARE... BE HIDING UNDER MY MOUNTAIN?

THIS WOULDN'T HAVE ANYTHING TO DO WITH A CERTAIN *PROPHECY,* WOULD IT?

WHAT'S GOING ON OUT HERE?

SCARLET!

WEBS! KESTREL!

KESTREL'S HERE, TOO? WHAT A *FUN* REUNION THIS IS GOING TO BE.

GO! HIDE!

DISAPPEAR WHILE YOU TRY TO DIE FOR US AGAIN? NO WAY.

THEY'RE THE DRAGONETS OF DESTINY! YOU HAVE TO LEAVE THEM ALONE!

BUT WHAT IF IT'S *MY* DESTINY TO PLAY WITH THEM?

CRACK!

DUNE!

I ALWAYS FIND THE ONES WHO BETRAY ME IN THE END. ISN'T THAT RIGHT, KESTREL?

YOU'VE GOT ME NOW. LET THESE WORTHLESS DRAGONETS GO.

WHY, KESTREL! HAVE YOU SWITCHED FROM DISOBEYING ORDERS TO GIVING THEM?

I'LL COME WITH YOU. JUST LEAVE THEM ALONE.

OF *COURSE* YOU'LL COME WITH ME. WE'VE GOT A THRILLING TRIAL PLANNED, FOLLOWED BY AN EVEN MORE THRILLING *EXECUTION*. AND THESE LITTLE DRAGONS... WILL BE PERFECT FOR MY ARENA.

TAKE THEM!

PART TWO: IN THE SKY KINGDOM

REALLY? ALL RIGHT. THAT'S THE QUEEN'S ARENA DOWN THERE.

THERE'S A BATTLE ALMOST EVERY DAY FOR HER MAJESTY'S AMUSEMENT. IF YOU WIN ENOUGH BATTLES, YOU GO FREE.

HOW MANY IS THAT?

I DON'T KNOW. NO ONE'S EVER DONE IT. AFTER A DRAGON HAS A FEW WINS, HER MAJESTY SENDS ME IN. I ALWAYS KILL THEM. I'M REALLY DANGEROUS.

I CAN'T WAIT TO FIGHT THE NIGHTWING! NOBODY KNOWS WHAT THAT WILL BE LIKE. WHAT IF HE CAN READ MY MIND AND KNOWS WHAT I'M GOING TO DO BEFORE I DO IT?

STARFLIGHT! WHERE IS HE?

SOMEWHERE OVER THERE.

WHAT ABOUT TSUNAMI?

THE SEAWING? BORING. I'VE FOUGHT PLENTY OF SEAWINGS.

HAVE YOU SEEN MY OTHER FRIENDS? GLORY, THE RAINWING? OR SUNNY? SHE'S SMALL AND KIND OF ODD-LOOKING AND —

HAVEN'T SEEN ANY DRAGONS LIKE THAT.

BUT I'LL KEEP AN EYE OUT IF YOU WANT.

CHEER FOR ME!

WELCOME TO TODAY'S BATTLE!

I DON'T WANT TO SEE THIS.

BUT I SHOULD LEARN HOW PERIL FIGHTS.

AFTER FOUR VICTORIES, HORIZON THE SANDWING—FORMERLY, AND UNWISELY, A SOLDIER IN BLAZE'S ARMY—HAS BEEN CHALLENGED TO A MATCH WITH THE QUEEN'S CHAMPION, PERIL.

HE'S BIGGER THAN HER! WHY IS HE AFRAID?

WHOOOSH!

AAAAH!

WHAT JUST HAPPENED? DOES SHE HAVE FIRE IN HER CLAWS?

AIYEEEEE!

AIYEEEEE!

SSSSSSSSSSSSSSS

SSSSSSSSSSSSSSSSS

FLUMPH!

WELL,
THAT WAS
BORING.

I HOPE TOMORROW
SOMEONE WILL AT LEAST
TRY TO AMUSE ME.
**TODAY'S GAMES
ARE OVER!**

OH, GOOD, NOW YOU'RE HUNGRY!

WHOA.

PLOP!

IT'S OKAY! I'LL STAY REALLY STILL, I PROMISE.

DO YOU WANT ANOTHER ONE?

I'M ALL RIGHT.

DO YOU WANT ME TO GO AWAY?

NO. STAY AND TALK TO ME.

AREN'T YOU AFRAID OF ME?

OF COURSE I AM. BUT YOU'RE STILL BETTER COMPANY THAN THE PIGEONS.

ALL *THEY* WANT TO TALK ABOUT IS WHO TO POOP ON.

HFN. SNORF! HEE!

ARE—ARE *YOU* ALL RIGHT?

UH?

I—

...

THAT WAS WEIRD TODAY. THE SANDWING—HE JUST GAVE UP. WHY WOULD HE DO THAT? HER MAJESTY WAS ANGRY.

ANGRY AT YOU? THAT DOESN'T SEEM FAIR.

IT DOESN'T?

NO, THE QUEEN IS RIGHT. IT'S MY RESPONSIBILITY TO MAKE THE FIGHT EXCITING.

WHY DO YOU DO WHAT SHE SAYS? DO YOU—LIKE FIGHTING?

OF COURSE. I'M GOOD AT FIGHTING.

SCARLET'S MY QUEEN. I'M HER CHAMPION.

PRIVATE AUDIENCE WITH THE QUEEN.

IS THAT A GOOD THING? OR A BAD THING?

SHUT UP.

I DON'T KNOW BECAUSE I'VE NEVER BEEN A PRISONER BEFORE. UNLESS, TECHNICALLY, MAYBE I WAS, BUT THIS IS A LOT... WINDIER. PLUS, THERE'S THE QUEEN, THAT'S NEW. DOES SHE NORMALLY MEET WITH PRISONERS? MAYBE RIGHT BEFORE LETTING THEM GO?

I SAID SHUT UP.

GRRRRRR...

KEEP HER STILL!

SHOULD I HAVE FOUGHT THEM, TOO?

BUT OUR WINGS ARE STILL CLAMPED... WE CAN'T FLY AWAY.

SHH!

HE'S TRYING TO TELL YOU THAT IT'S **RUDE** TO TALK TO ANYONE BEFORE THE QUEEN IN HER OWN THRONE ROOM. WHAT **DO** THEY TEACH DRAGONETS THESE DAYS? **BOW.**

SORRY.

OOF! LET ME **GO!**

THIS IS AN OUTRAGE! WE'RE THE—

DRAGONETS OF DESTINY, YES, VERY THRILLING.

YOU KNOW, NOT EVERYONE **WANTS** THIS WAR TO END. PERSONALLY, I LOVE IT.

I GET LOTS OF CONTENDERS FOR THE ARENA FROM THE BATTLEFIELD.

AND IT'S A TERRIFIC DISTRACTION FOR DRAGONS WHO MIGHT HAVE CHALLENGED ME FOR THE THRONE. SAVES ME A LOT OF TROUBLE.

SO IT'S ALL RIGHT WITH YOU THAT DRAGONS HAVE *DIED* ALL OVER THE WORLD?

AS IF *YOU* KNOW ANYTHING ABOUT THAT.

HAVE *YOU* EVER BEEN IN A REAL BATTLE? HAVE *YOU* EVER SEEN HUNDREDS OF DEAD DRAGONS? DO YOU KNOW *ANYTHING*, REALLY, ABOUT THIS WAR?

WE'VE STUDIED IT...

WE KNOW IT'S AWFUL...

INNOCENT DRAGONS ARE GETTING HURT!

IT'S EASY TO *SAY* WAR IS AWFUL, BUT HARD TO SOLVE OUR DRAGON PROBLEMS WITHOUT ONE.

WHO *SHOULD* BE THE NEXT SANDWING QUEEN? BURN, BLISTER, OR BLAZE?

I'D *LOVE* TO KNOW WHAT YOU'VE DECIDED FROM THE WISDOM OF YOUR UNDERGROUND CAVE.

THAT WASN'T OUR FAULT! WE **WANTED** TO BE OUT IN THE WORLD.

THAT'S WHAT YOU THINK. HILARIOUS. AS IF YOU'D HAVE SURVIVED THIS LONG OUT THERE.

YOUR GUARDIANS **DID** TELL YOU WHAT HAPPENED TO ALL THE SKYWING DRAGONETS BORN ON THE BRIGHTEST NIGHT, DIDN'T THEY?

I WON'T GO INTO DETAILS, BUT IT WAS VERY SAD.

EXCUSE ME! I HAVE A QUESTION, YOUR MAJESTY.

WHERE'S SUNNY? IS SHE ALL RIGHT?

STOMP!

OH, THE ODD-LOOKING SANDWING. I THINK BURN WILL LIKE HER VERY MUCH.

SHE COLLECTS CURIOSITIES. YOU SHOULD SEE HER PALACE. IT'S QUITE HORRIFYING.

FULL OF TWO-HEADED LIZARDS...

...AND SEVEN-TOED DRAGON TALONS...

...AND STUFFED SCAVENGERS WITH WEIRD PALE SKIN...

...YOUR LITTLE FRIEND WILL FIT RIGHT IN.

YOU CAN'T GIVE SUNNY TO BURN!

I CAN DO WHATEVER I LIKE.

WHAT'S WRONG WITH GLORY?

NOTHING. SHE'S QUITE PERFECT, IF YOU ASK ME.

WHY IS SHE ALL... SLEEPY?

RAINWINGS ARE NATURALLY LAZY. HADN'T YOU NOTICED? BUT THEN, MUDWINGS ARE NATURALLY STUPID.

YOU HAVE TO LET US GO! THE PROPHECY—

OH, SHUSH. YOUR SPUNKINESS IS STARTING TO BORE ME. MY HATCHING DAY IS TOMORROW, AND I WANT A THRILLING ARENA.

BUT I WANT TO SEE AT LEAST ONE OF YOU FIGHT TODAY. SO WHICH OF YOU IS MOST LIKELY TO SURVIVE? THE NIGHTWING?

ME!

ADORABLE. BUT SERIOUSLY.

YOU'RE DELUSIONAL. I BEAT YOU ALL THE TIME.

A MUDWING WOULD BE MORE EXCITING THAN JUST ANOTHER SEAWING, WOULDN'T IT?

I LOVE YOUR ENTHUSIASM, DRAGONETS!

GUARDS, TAKE *THESE* TWO AWAY.

AS FOR THIS ONE... PREPARE HIM FOR THE ARENA.

AFTER LAST MONTH'S BATTLE WITH BLAZE'S ARMY, MY DUNGEONS WERE STUFFED WITH ICEWING PRISONERS OF WAR. ONLY FIVE HAVE SURVIVED. AFTER TWO WINS, HERE'S—FJORD OF THE ICEWINGS!

AND IN THIS CORNER: I'M SURE A LEGENDARY DRAGONET OF DESTINY WILL HAVE NO PROBLEM SURVIVING MY LITTLE ARENA. ISN'T THAT RIGHT, CLAY OF THE MUDWINGS?

KILL THE MUDWING!

WHOOO!

RIP HIS TALONS OFF!

HUZZAH!

FREEZE OFF HIS FACE!

BURN HIM UP!

KILL THE ICEWING!

CLAWS UP! TEETH READY! FIGHT!

EVISCERATE!

SHOVE HIS TAIL DOWN HIS THROAT!

I REALLY DIDN'T THINK THIS PLAN THROUGH...

STOP. PERIL, IT WASN'T ME.

IT'S ALL RIGHT. I'D KEEP IT SECRET, TOO.

ARE YOU OKAY?

MY WING'S A LITTLE STIFF.

IT CAN'T BE THAT BAD. I'VE BEEN HURT BEFORE.

GASP

NOT BY AN ICEWING, I BET.

IT FEELS BETTER WITH YOU NEAR IT. YOUR HEAT, I MEAN.

OH! I KNOW WHAT TO GET. WAIT HERE.

BECAUSE I WAS GOING TO GO WHERE? FOR A WALK?

THIS WILL HEAL YOU. SPREAD YOUR WING.

IS THAT MUD?

IT HEALS MUDWINGS. I DON'T KNOW WHY I DIDN'T THINK OF IT BEFORE.

WHAT ARE YOU DOING?

I CAN'T RUB IT ON YOU. YOU'D BURN UP.

OH. RIGHT.

HAVE YOU EVER THOUGHT ABOUT LEAVING?

I'M NOT ALLOWED. I'VE NEVER BEEN OUTSIDE THE SKY KINGDOM.

SPLAT!

WHY NOT? YOU MUST BE THE MOST POWERFUL DRAGON HERE.

I WOULD NEVER DISOBEY HER MAJESTY!

BESIDES, I HAVE TO EAT THE BLACK ROCKS EVERY DAY, OR I'LL DIE.

SPLAT!

BLACK ROCKS?

IT'S PART OF THE CURSE OF HAVING TOO MUCH FIRE. THEY'RE REALLY RARE. I'M LUCKY QUEEN SCARLET GETS THEM FOR ME.

HAVE YOU EVER TRIED NOT EATING THEM?

ONCE, WHEN I WAS A LOT YOUNGER. I GOT MAD AT HER MAJESTY BECAUSE SHE WOULDN'T TELL ME ANYTHING ABOUT MY MOTHER. SO I STOPPED EATING THEM AND I GOT SICK.

LIKE, *DYING* SICK.

QUEEN SCARLET CARES ENOUGH TO KEEP ME ALIVE. MY MOTHER DIDN'T.

IS THAT WHY YOU DON'T CHALLENGE HER FOR THE THRONE?

THAT'S AWFUL! I DON'T WANT TO BE QUEEN. STOP SAYING TREASONOUS THINGS!

FZZZZZZZZZZZ!

YAA!

FEEL BETTER?

YEAH!

THANKS.

QUICK, SPREAD YOUR WINGS! I DON'T WANT ANYONE TO SEE ME!

WAA—? WHAT, WHY?

THEY'RE HAVING A TRIAL, AND QUEEN SCARLET SAID I WASN'T ALLOWED TO WATCH! I *NEVER* GO TO TRIALS. THEY'RE BORING. SO WHY WOULD SHE TELL ME I CAN'T GO?

SOMETHING'S GOING ON, AND I WANT TO SEE WHAT IT IS.

REMEMBER, YOU *OWE* ME. I BROUGHT YOU THE MUD.

IT'S OKAY, PERIL. I'D HELP YOU ANYWAY.

OH, I FOUND YOUR SANDWING.

SUNNY! WHERE IS SHE?

IF YOU HIDE ME, I'LL TELL YOU. BUT IF YOU TURN ME IN, I WON'T.

PERIL, I TOLD YOU, I'D HELP YOU WHETHER—*SIGH*. OKAY. BUT WON'T SOMEONE BE LOOKING FOR YOU?

NOT TODAY. I'M SUPPOSED TO BE DOWN IN THE CAVES LOOKING FOR BLACK ROCKS.

WHY DOES QUEEN SCARLET BOTHER WITH TRIALS?

SHE LIKES THE DRAMA OF THEM.

THEY'RE STARTING!

THAT'S VERMILION, QUEEN SCARLET'S OLDEST SON. HE ALWAYS ARGUES FOR THE PROSECUTION.

YOU LOOK PARTICULARLY DEADLY TODAY, YOUR MAJESTY.

YES, YES, I KNOW I DO.

AND THE OLD ONE'S OSPREY. HE LOST HIS WINGS IN THE WAR. HE'S MY FRIEND, BUT HE TALKS LIKE A SCROLL.

SO DOES MY FRIEND STARFLIGHT.

WHERE'S OUR DEFENDANT? SOMEONE FETCH HER!

RRRRRR!

GRAWWR!

KESTREL!

YOU KNOW HER?

SHE'S ONE OF THE DRAGONS WHO RAISED US. THEY DIDN'T LIKE US MUCH, BUT THEY KEPT US ALIVE.

I GUESS EVEN TERRIBLE PARENTS ARE BETTER THAN NO PARENTS.

LOYAL SUBJECTS! THIS DRAGON, KESTREL, STANDS ACCUSED OF HIGHEST TREASON —DISOBEYING ME.

YOUR MAJESTY, THE FACTS ARE CLEAR. YOU GAVE AN ORDER. KESTREL DISOBEYED YOU. SHE DESERVES A LONG AND PAINFUL EXECUTION.

VERY COMPELLING. WELL SAID. SOUNDS GUILTY TO ME.

YOUR MAJESTY. I DO HAVE A FEW WORDS TO SAY IN THIS PRISONER'S DEFENSE.

IF YOU MUST.

YOU ORDERED KESTREL TO DESTROY HER EGG. IT WAS A SINGLE EGG, BUT INSIDE THERE WERE TWO DRAGONETS. ONE HAD NO FIRE AT ALL, BUT THE OTHER—

HAD TOO MUCH.

TOO MUCH FIRE? LIKE YOU?

NO OTHER DRAGONETS LIKE ME HAVE HATCHED IN YEARS AND YEARS...

IS KESTREL... YOUR MOTHER?

MY MOTHER IS DEAD! QUEEN SCARLET KILLED HER TO SAVE ME!

MAYBE THAT WAS A LIE.

WE *KNOW* ALL THIS. SKIP TO THE PART WHERE WE EXECUTE HER.

YOU ORDERED HER TO DESTROY THE DEFECTIVE EGG. HOWEVER, SHE FLED WITH IT—

NO! MY BROTHER DIED IN THE EGG! I KILLED HIM!

AND MY *MOTHER* TRIED TO KILL *ME*!

SCARLET IS THE ONE WHO SAVED ME!

AT LEAST, THAT'S WHAT SHE TOLD YOU.

YOU ADMIT KESTREL DISOBEYED ME. I THINK WE'RE DONE HERE.

BUT SHE *TRIED* TO OBEY YOU. YOU'RE THE ONE WHO REVERSED YOUR ORDER.

I CHANGED MY MIND. I'M THE QUEEN. I CAN DO THAT.

KESTREL WAS ALWAYS A FAITHFUL SOLDIER TO YOU. SHE FOLLOWED YOUR ORDERS, AND WHAT DID YOU DO? ORDERED HER TO KILL HER OWN DRAGONETS!

ENOUGH! WE'LL EXECUTE HER TOMORROW. AND WHILE WE'RE AT IT, EXECUTE HIM, TOO, FOR BORING ME.

WHO KEPT YOU ALIVE ALL THESE YEARS? FINDING YOU BLACK ROCKS, FEEDING YOU, MAKING YOU MY OWN ROYAL CHAMPION? AREN'T I A BETTER MOTHER THAN HER ANYWAY?

I CALL UPON THE TRADITION OF THE CHAMPION'S SHIELD. I WANT TO FIGHT FOR MY MOTHER.

WHAT?

AS QUEEN'S CHAMPION, I CAN STAND FOR ANY CONDEMNED DRAGON. IF I WIN MY NEXT FIGHT, YOU HAVE TO LET HER GO.

NOW WHERE DID *YOU* HEAR ABOUT *THAT* OLD LAW?

YOU.

STOP!

WHAT ARE WE GOING TO DO?

STARFLIGHT WON'T SURVIVE THE ARENA TOMORROW...

AND BURN IS COMING FOR SUNNY...

IS THAT PERIL...?

NO.

CAN WE SAVE KESTREL?

STARFLIGHT AND SUNNY WON'T MAKE IT...

PLEASE, PERIL... COME ON...

THINK ABOUT SOMETHING ELSE.

THINK ABOUT COWS.

MMMM, COWS.

I WISH I COULD SHARE A COW WITH MY FRIENDS RIGHT NOW.

I MISS THEM.

PERIL! FINALLY!

THAT'S NOT PERIL.

THAT'S
BURN...

YOU INTERRUPTED MY FEAST. YOU WILL *NOT* DO SO AGAIN.

WHY DON'T WE JUST KILL THEM?

THAT WOULDN'T BE FUN.

WE HAVE A WHOLE DAY OF ENTERTAINMENT PLANNED FOR TOMORROW. IT'S MY HATCHING DAY! I WANT IT TO BE THRILLING.

I DON'T CARE ABOUT YOUR "FUN." WE NEED TO STOP THE PROPHECY. LET'S KILL THEM AND GET IT OVER WITH.

WELL... YES. BUT THINK. IF WE KILL THE DRAGONETS NOW, OUT OF SIGHT, IT DOES US NO GOOD.

EVEN IF WE HANG THEM FROM THE PALACE WALLS, NO ONE WILL BELIEVE IT'S THEM.

BUT IF WE PUT THE DRAGONETS IN THE ARENA, *EVERYONE* CAN *SEE* THEM DIE.

THEY'LL LOSE ALL FAITH IN THE PROPHECY. *MUCH* MORE POWERFUL THAT WAY, WITH GRUESOME VISUALS!

DON'T YOU AGREE?

WHAT IF THEY WIN?

THEY WON'T.

BUT KILLING THEM OURSELVES IS A SOLID BACKUP PLAN.

YOU KNOW WE'RE *RIGHT HERE*, RIGHT? DON'T YOU WANT TO HATCH YOUR EVIL PLANS SOMEWHERE MORE SECRETIVE?

WHO DO YOU THINK YOU'LL TELL BEFORE YOU DIE?

YIPES!

WHOOSH

I THOUGHT I'D GET TO PLAY WITH YOU LONGER, BUT I GUESS YOU ALL HAVE TO DIE TOMORROW. NOBODY LETS ME HAVE ANY FUN.

SLEEP WELL, SO YOU'LL BE *THRILLING* FOR MY ARENA.

I DON'T LIKE THEM.

OW!

I'M SO GLAD YOU'RE ALIVE! YOU INCREDIBLY HUGE IDIOT.

SO AM I. BUT I'M MORE GLAD YOU TWO ARE ALIVE.

PLAYING THAT SONG WAS PRETTY SMART, TSUNAMI.

?

I THOUGHT *YOU DID THAT!*

HER CAGE IS IN QUEEN BURN'S GUEST CHAMBERS. I CAN SNEAK IN AND GET HER TOMORROW DURING THE ARENA FIGHTS.

OH, THANK YOU!

OOPS— CAREFUL.

WHAT ABOUT CLAY AND STARFLIGHT? I CAN SURVIVE THE ARENA, BUT WE HAVE TO GET THEM OUT OF IT.

I CAN SURVIVE THE ARENA! HELLO, I ALREADY HAVE.

RIGHT, AND HOW DID YOU DO THAT? I HAPPEN TO KNOW YOU DON'T HAVE SECRET VENOM IN YOUR CLAWS.

I... OK, I HAVE NO IDEA WHERE THE VENOM CAME FROM.

HMM. MAYBE IT WAS SCARLET, TRYING TO KEEP THINGS INTERESTING?

I KNOW WHAT TO DO!

IN THE ARENA?

TO GET US OUT OF HERE! PERIL, THE FIRE DOESN'T HURT YOU! COULD YOU PICK UP THE ROCKS AND MOVE THEM? SO WE CAN GET OUT?

YOU ARE SMART.

I SUPPOSE I COULD DO THAT.

IF YOU'RE REALLY SURE YOU WANT TO ESCAPE TONIGHT.

OF COURSE WE ARE! WE CAN HIDE SOMEWHERE UNTIL YOU FREE SUNNY TOMORROW.

WE'D BE REALLY GRATEFUL.

AND GLORY. WE'LL FIGURE OUT HOW TO SAVE GLORY, TOO.

WHO'S GLORY?

STOP MAKING HER MAD!

ME? WHAT DID I DO?

WELL, YOU'RE A HANDSOME IDIOT.

SHE HAS A CRUSH ON YOU.

SHE DOES?

IT'S PRETTY OBVIOUS.

AND SHE DEFINITELY *DOESN'T* WANT TO HEAR YOU TALK ABOUT LEAVING. OR ABOUT RESCUING OTHER GIRLS.

READY TO CLIMB?

PERIL, LOOK OUT! IT'S THE QUEEN!

YOU CAN'T BE SEEN WITH US. SHE'LL KILL YOU! YOU HAVE TO HIDE!

WHY—
WHY AREN'T YOU
BURNING UP?

SO, YOU'VE
FINALLY FIGURED
IT OUT.

MUDWINGS HATCHED
FROM BLOOD-RED EGGS
HAVE FIREPROOF SCALES.

DIDN'T
THE TALONS OF
PEACE TEACH YOU
ANYTHING?

BUT...
KESTREL
USED TO
BURN ME IN
THE CAVE...

REMEMBER
HOW QUICKLY
YOU HEALED,
THOUGH?

THANK YOU,
PERIL. YOU MAY
BE EXCUSED.

THANK
YOU...?

PERIL TURNED
US IN! I KNEW WE
COULDN'T TRUST HER!

GUARDS!
LOCK THEM
UP!

BUT FIRST, LET ME WELCOME OUR HONORED GUEST, QUEEN BURN OF THE SANDWINGS!

A RAINWING PET? THIS IS A FRIVOLOUS KINGDOM.

CAREFUL WHAT YOU SAY TO YOUR ALLIES.

FIRST, WE HAVE A SO-CALLED DRAGONET OF DESTINY. CAN SHE FULFILL THE PROPHECY? LET'S SEE IF SHE CAN SURVIVE THE ARENA FIRST.

I GIVE YOU... **TSUNAMI OF THE SEAWINGS!**

DISAPPOINTING.

CATASTROPHIC. LOOK, THE IDIOTS LOVE HER NOW.

DON'T WORRY, I HAVE A PLAN.

HURRAH!

BUT NOW IT'S TIME FOR THE NIGHTWING! MY HATCHING DAY PRESENT TO ME!

WAIT! LET ME FIGHT FOR HIM INSTEAD!

THESE DRAGONETS. CONSTANTLY PUSHING AND SHOVING TO SAVE EACH OTHER. IT'S THE WEIRDEST THING.

MMM.

THE RAREST OF ALL DRAGONS—A REAL LIVE NIGHTWING! LET'S SEE WHAT HAPPENS WHEN TWO DRAGONETS OF DESTINY HAVE TO FIGHT EACH OTHER!

GUARDS! BRING IN THE ICEWINGS!

FINALLY A SMART IDEA.

UNCHAIN THEM ALL! FOUR ICEWINGS SHOULDN'T BE TOO MUCH FOR THE FAMOUS DRAGONETS OF DESTINY!

PUT ME IN WITH THEM! LET ME FIGHT, TOO!

WHAT ABOUT THE REST OF US?

OURS WHO? WE FOUND HIM WITH THE TALONS OF PEACE.

HAVE THE NIGHTWINGS CHOSEN A SIDE? ARE YOU ALLYING WITH TRAITORS NOW?

MORROWSEER, OVER HERE! DRAGONETS OF DESTINY!

NO. I COME TO CLAIM THIS DRAGONET AS OURS. WE WILL TAKE HIM AND GO.

OH, *WILL* YOU?

DO NOT ANGER THE NIGHTWINGS, SKY DRAGON.

COME ON!

CAN'T YOU HEAR ME?

WE NEED HELP!

THERE. WE'VE TAKEN CARE OF YOUR ICEWING PROBLEM. NOW WE'LL TAKE OUR DRAGONET AND GO.

ON BEHALF OF THE PRISONER KESTREL, MY CHAMPION PERIL HAS ASKED TO FIGHT A DRAGON OF MY CHOOSING.

IF PERIL WINS, KESTREL GOES FREE.

IF SHE LOSES—THEN I SUPPOSE I'LL HAVE TO GET A NEW CHAMPION.

I KNOW: YOU THINK PERIL *CAN'T* LOSE.

WELL, IT SO HAPPENS WE HAVE HERE TODAY A DRAGON WHOSE SCALES ARE IMPERVIOUS TO FIRE!

UH-OH.

ISN'T THAT... *THRILLING?*

HAHHH!

OOF!

PERIL, IT DOESN'T HAVE TO BE LIKE THIS. WE DON'T HAVE TO KILL EACH OTHER.

WE DO!

DRAGONS KILL EACH OTHER ALL THE TIME. THAT'S HOW WE ARE.

ESPECIALLY YOU AND ME. WE'RE THE SAME.

WE WERE KILLERS FROM THE MOMENT WE HATCHED!

THAT'S NOT WHO I WANT TO BE.

MAYBE THAT'S WHAT THE PROPHECY IS ABOUT. MAYBE WE'RE SUPPOSED TO SHOW EVERYONE HOW TO GET ALONG WITHOUT ALL THE KILLING.

HURRY UP AND DO IT!

USE YOUR VENOM! I DIDN'T EVEN GET TO SEE IT THE FIRST TIME!

GLORY! YOU'RE AWAKE!

OF COURSE I AM! COULDN'T YOU TELL I WAS FAKING? YOU SERIOUSLY THOUGHT I WAS ASLEEP THIS WHOLE TIME?

UH —

YOU *LOOKED* PRETTY ASLEEP.

WELL, THAT'S *GREAT*.

FOR THE FIRST TIME IN MY LIFE, I *PRETEND* TO BE AS LAZY AS EVERYONE SAYS RAINWINGS ARE, AND YOU *ACTUALLY* BELIEVE IT.

SO GLAD MY FRIENDS HAVE SO MUCH FAITH IN ME.

WE HAVE TO GET OUT OF HERE. GLORY SCARED BURN OFF, BUT SHE WON'T STAY GONE LONG.

CLAY, WAIT!

SIZZLE

THANKS, PERIL. NOW MY FRIENDS?

PLEASE. IF WE'RE REALLY FRIENDS.

...

ALL RIGHT.

CHNK!

NOW TAKE US TO SUNNY.

FSSSSSS

GLORY, YOU NEVER TOLD US YOU COULD SHOOT VENOM!

I NEVER COULD BEFORE.

BUT *HOW* DID YOU DO IT?

OH, WELL, THERE'S A LOGICAL SCIENTIFIC EXPLANATION AND, *SERIOUSLY, RIGHT NOW* YOU WANT TO HAVE THIS CONVERSATION?

SUNNY!

I *KNEW* YOU'D BE ALL RIGHT! I JUST KEPT THINKING ABOUT THE PROPHECY AND HOW WE CAN'T DIE BECAUSE WE HAVE TO STOP THE WAR!

SIZZLE!

SNAP!

WAIT... WHERE'S STARFLIGHT?

HE'S ALL RIGHT. ESCAPE NOW, EXPLAIN LATER.

CLAY, WAIT. MY MOTHER! IF QUEEN SCARLET ISN'T DEAD, SHE'LL KILL HER.

YOU'RE RIGHT. WE HAVE TO GET KESTREL OUT.

WHY? WHAT DO WE CARE?

WE CARE. WE CAN'T HELP IT. SHE RAISED US.

I DON'T. SHE WAS GOING TO KILL ME.

SHE DIDN'T RAISE US TO CARE ABOUT HER. SHE RAISED US TO STAY ALIVE.

PERIL?

WHAT ARE YOU DOING HERE?

RESCUING YOU. AGAINST MY WILL.

STAND BACK.

FSSSSS

I... I THOUGHT YOU WERE DEAD.

I THOUGHT YOU WERE DEAD.

BUT I GUESS I DIDN'T NEED YOU. I TURNED OUT ALL RIGHT.

ALL RIGHT?

QUEEN SCARLET TOOK CARE OF ME. SHE KEPT ME SAFE AND FOUND ME BLACK ROCKS. SHE GAVE ME A PURPOSE.

BLACK ROCKS?

HEY! THE PRISONERS!

RUN.

STUPID WORM!

THAT GUARD WILL RAISE THE ALARM. WE'LL BE CAUGHT IN MOMENTS.

DON'T TALK TO CLAY THAT WAY! JUST—FOLLOW US AND STOP TALKING.

LET'S FIND GLORY AND SUNNY AT THE RIVER.

STAY LOW, WE DON'T WANT TO BE SEEN.

OH, COULD I BE?

"THE LARGEST EGG IN MOUNTAIN HIGH." IF YOU HATCHED WITH A TWIN, YOUR EGG MUST HAVE BEEN *HUGE.*

WOW. DO YOU THINK SO?

THAT'S TRUE! MAYBE I'M PART OF YOUR DESTINY!

NOT A CHANCE. PERIL HATCHED OVER A YEAR BEFORE THE BRIGHTEST NIGHT.

YOUR SKYWING DIED IN THE EGG. I SAW THE SHATTERED SHELL.

COME WITH ME. I'M NOT MUCH, BUT I'M BETTER THAN SCARLET.

I CAN'T GO WITH EITHER OF YOU. HOW WOULD I GET MY BLACK ROCKS?

TELL ME ABOUT THESE BLACK ROCKS.

YOU KNOW, THE ROCKS! I HAVE TO EAT THEM EVERY DAY TO STAY ALIVE.

MORE OF SCARLET'S LIES. YOU DON'T NEED ANYTHING LIKE THAT.

BUT—I STOPPED TAKING THEM AND GOT SICK—

POISON IN YOUR FOOD. ONE OF SCARLET'S FAVORITE TRICKS.

WAS ANYTHING SHE TOLD ME TRUE?

SCARLET? I DOUBT IT.

IT'S OKAY, CLAY. SHE DOESN'T REALLY MEAN IT.

YEAH. SHE DOES.

YOU CAN STILL COME WITH US. EVEN IF YOU'RE NOT IN THE PROPHECY.

NO. I DON'T THINK...

I DON'T THINK I DESERVE TO.

WHAT DOES THAT MEAN?

IT'S LIKE YOU SAID. THERE ARE DRAGONS THEY WRITE PROPHECIES ABOUT... AND THEN THERE'S ME.

PART THREE: AN EGG THE COLOR OF DRAGON BLOOD

YOU CAN'T GO IN ALONE!

THE MUDWINGS WON'T TRUST THE FOUR OF US, ALL TOGETHER.

IT'S TRUE. *ESPECIALLY* TSUNAMI. THE SEAWINGS ARE ON BLISTER'S SIDE.

AND WHO *KNOWS* WHAT THEY'D THINK OF SUNNY?

IF I DON'T COME BACK BY SUNRISE, COME LOOK FOR ME.

WHAT IF YOU NEED US BEFORE THEN?

I'LL GO WITH YOU, CLAY.

NO ONE WOULD CARE I'M A RAINWING SINCE THEY'RE NOT IN THE WAR.

BUT, I CAN ALSO DO

THIS.

I THINK YOU'RE STILL TOO PRETTY TO BE A MUDWING.

NONSENSE. YOU'RE JUST AS PRETTY AS GLORY, CLAY.

DEFINITELY!

I'M NOT SURE HOW TO TAKE THAT.

WE'LL WAIT BY THE RIVER. BE SAFE.

WE'RE JUST LOOKING FOR SOMEONE. A MUDWING COUPLE WHO LOST AN EGG SIX YEARS AGO.

A MUDWING COUPLE?

THERE WAS A RED EGG. IT WAS STOLEN FROM AROUND HERE.

STOLEN!

OR TAKEN ANYWAY? MAYBE BY A DRAGON NAMED ASHA?

OH, YOU MUST BE TALKING ABOUT ASHA'S SISTER CATTAIL. SHE HAD A BLOOD EGG ABOUT SIX YEARS BACK. BUT IT WASN'T STOLEN.

CATTAIL! IS SHE ALL RIGHT? IS SHE STILL ALIVE?

SOMEHOW. THAT TROOP HAS NO DISCIPLINE. THEY'RE DOWN TO FOUR NOW.

WHERE CAN WE FIND HER?

THEY BUNK IN THE BROKEN SLEEPHOUSE AT THE END OF THE PATH.

THANKS.

HAVE YOU NOTICED NO ONE'S PAYING ATTENTION TO US?

I HAVE A THEORY ABOUT THAT.

THE SCROLLS WE HAD ON THE MUDWINGS WERE NEVER ANY GOOD. BUT YOU SEE THESE GROUPS OF DRAGONS FLYING AROUND?

MAYBE THEY'RE LIKE ARMY TROOPS.

THEIR ARMY'S MADE UP OF THESE SMALL, LOYAL UNITS.

MAYBE THAT'S WHAT MAKES THEM SUCH GOOD FIGHTERS.

DOES THIS MEAN THEY WANT THE COWS BACK? BECAUSE THEY CAN'T HAVE THEM.

YOU *SOLD* ME?

WHY NOT? THERE WERE SIX OTHER EGGS IN THE HATCHING. THEY DIDN'T NEED YOU.

WHAT ABOUT MY *FATHER*? DIDN'T HE TRY TO STOP YOU?

HEE! SNORF! YOU DON'T KNOW *ANYTHING* ABOUT MUDWINGS, DO YOU? YOUR FATHER DOESN'T CARE.

I DON'T EVEN KNOW WHO HE IS. THE TRIBE HAS BREEDING NIGHTS ONCE A MONTH, NOTHING MORE.

...NO FATHER?

AND NO MOTHER EITHER, APPARENTLY.

THAT'S RIGHT. GOOD LUCK, BUT THERE'S NO ROOM IN OUR TROOP FOR CLINGY DRAGONETS.

WE HEARD YOU WERE ASKING ABOUT CATTAIL'S BLOOD EGG.

THAT'S RIGHT.

WHAT HAPPENED TO IT? DO YOU KNOW? DID IT HATCH?

WHO'S ASKING?

I'M REED.

THIS IS SORA,

PHEASANT,

MARSH,

AND UMBER.

DID ONE OF YOU HATCH FROM THE BLOOD EGG? ARE YOU OUR MISSING SIB?

SIB...?

SIBLING? IS THAT WHAT YOU MEAN? WERE WE IN THE SAME HATCHING?

I *KNEW* IT! I *KNEW* HE FELT FAMILIAR! I *TOLD* YOU!

YOU'RE OUR BROTHER. YOU SHOULD HAVE BEEN WITH US ALL ALONG.

HE'S NOT *JUST* OUR BROTHER.

LOOK AT THE *SIZE* OF HIM! HE SHOULD BE OUR BIGWINGS.

OH. THAT'S TRUE.

ER...

WHAT'S A BIGWINGS?

MUDWING NESTS ARE REALLY SAFE, SO MOTHERS DON'T CHECK ON THEM OFTEN, YOU KNOW? WE USUALLY HATCH ALONE.

THE FIRST HATCHED IS ALWAYS THE BIGGEST.

THAT'S WHY HE'S THE BIGWINGS!

THE FIRST THING A BIGWINGS DOES IS HELP HIS SIBS HATCH BY CRACKING OPEN THEIR SHELLS.

CLAY! YOU KNOW WHAT THIS MEANS? YOU *DIDN'T* TRY TO KILL US. YOU WERE HELPING US!

I WAS...?

THEN THE BIGWINGS TAKES CARE OF EVERYONE!

SOME BIGWINGS ARE MEAN OR BOSSY, BUT REED'S *GREAT*.

WE HUNT TOGETHER, WE SLEEP TOGETHER, WE FIGHT TOGETHER...

OH, SORRY...

DID YOU — DID WE LOSE SOMEONE?

OUR SISTER. CRANE.

TWO DAYS AGO IN THE BATTLE BY THE RIVER.

ONE OF THOSE DRAGONS WAS MY *SISTER.*

I WAS NOT THE BIGWINGS I WANTED TO BE.

YOU WERE AMAZING, REED.

WE'D *ALL* BE DEAD IF IT WEREN'T FOR YOU.

THERE
THEY ARE!

STARFLIGHT!

...GLORY?

OH—

YUP.
IT'S ME.

MORROWSEER
JUST DROPPED
HIM ON US FROM
THE SKY. ISN'T
THAT GREAT?

NIGHTWINGS.
EVER SO HELPFUL
AND NEVER
INFURIATINGLY
CRYPTIC AT
ALL.

I TRIED TO MAKE HIM BRING ME
BACK RIGHT AWAY, BUT HE WOULDN'T
LET ME GO. HE SAID THEY COULDN'T
AFFORD TO LOSE ANY NIGHTWINGS,
EVEN "PECULIAR LITTLE ONES."

YOU'RE NOT
PECULIAR! I'M
THE ONE WHO'S
PECULIAR.

WHAT DID
YOU LEARN IN THE
MUD KINGDOM? DID
YOU MEET CLAY'S
MOTHER?

...

THE **IMPORTANT** THING WE LEARNED IS THAT CLAY WASN'T TRYING TO KILL OUR EGGS. HE WAS *TRYING TO HELP US HATCH!*

I NEVER THOUGHT YOU *WERE* TRYING TO KILL US.

AS IF YOU EVER WOULD!

IT DID SEEM UNLIKELY.

WELL, *I* DIDN'T KNOW THAT.

SO WHAT NOW, BIGWINGS?

WE'LL BE LIKE THE MUDWINGS.

DISCOVER THE EPIC SERIES WHERE IT ALL BEGAN!

TUI T. SUTHERLAND

THE *NEW YORK TIMES* BESTSELLING SERIES

WINGS OF FIRE

THE HIDDEN KINGDOM

TUI T. SUTHERLAND

THE *NEW YORK TIMES* BESTSELLING SERIES

WINGS OF FIRE

THE DARK SECRET

TUI T. SUTHERLAND

THE *NEW YORK TIMES* BESTSELLING SERIES

WINGS OF FIRE

THE BRIGHTEST NIGHT

TUI T. SUTHERLAND

THE *NEW YORK TIMES* BESTSELLING SERIES

WINGS OF FIRE

ESCAPING PERIL

TUI T. SUTHERLAND

THE *NEW YORK TIMES* BESTSELLING SERIES

WINGS OF FIRE

TALONS OF POWER

TUI T. SUTHERLAND

THE *NEW YORK TIMES* BESTSELLING SERIES

WINGS OF FIRE

DARKNESS OF DRAGONS

EBOOK ORIGINALS

TUI T. SUTHERLAND

THE *NEW YORK TIMES* BESTSELLING SERIES

WINGS OF FIRE

WINGLETS #1 – PRISONERS

TUI T. SUTHERLAND

THE *NEW YORK TIMES* BESTSELLING SERIES

WINGS OF FIRE

WINGLETS #2 – ASSASSIN

TUI T. SUTHERLAND

THE *NEW YORK TIMES* BESTSELLING SERIES

WINGS OF FIRE

WINGLETS #3 – DESERTER

TUI T. SUTHERLAND

THE *NEW YORK TIMES* BESTSELLING SERIES

WINGS OF FIRE

WINGLETS #4 – RUNAWAY

TUI T. SUTHERLAND is the author of the *New York Times* and *USA Today* bestselling Wings of Fire series, the Menagerie trilogy, and the Pet Trouble series, as well as a contributing author to the bestselling Spirit Animals and Seekers series (as part of the Erin Hunter team). In 2009, she was a two-day champion on *Jeopardy!* She lives in Massachusetts with her wonderful husband, two adorable sons, and two very patient dogs. To learn more about Tui's books, visit her online at www.tuibooks.com.

BARRY DEUTSCH is an award-winning cartoonist and the creator of the Hereville series of graphic novels, about yet another troll-fighting 11-year-old Orthodox Jewish girl. He lives in Portland, Oregon, with a variable number of cats and fish.

MIKE HOLMES has drawn for the comics series Bravest Warriors and Adventure Time and is the creator of the art project *Mikenesses*. His books include *Secret Coders* (written by Gene Luen Yang), *Animal Crackers: Circus Mayhem* (written by Scott Christian Sava), and the *True Story* collection. He lives in Philadelphia with his wife, Meredith; Heidi the dog; and Ella the cat.

MAARTA LAIHO spends her days and nights as a comic colorist, where her work includes the comics series Lumberjanes, Adventure Time, and The Mighty Zodiac. When she's not doing that, she can be found hoarding houseplants and talking to her cat. She lives in the woods of Maine.